SAMPLE COLORING PAGES

FREE COLORING PAGES!

Check out: **SwearWordColoringBook.com** for FREE swear word coloring pages.

Don't forget to sign up to my mailing list for news, updates, and future FREE coloring pages!

Need EXTRA stress relief?

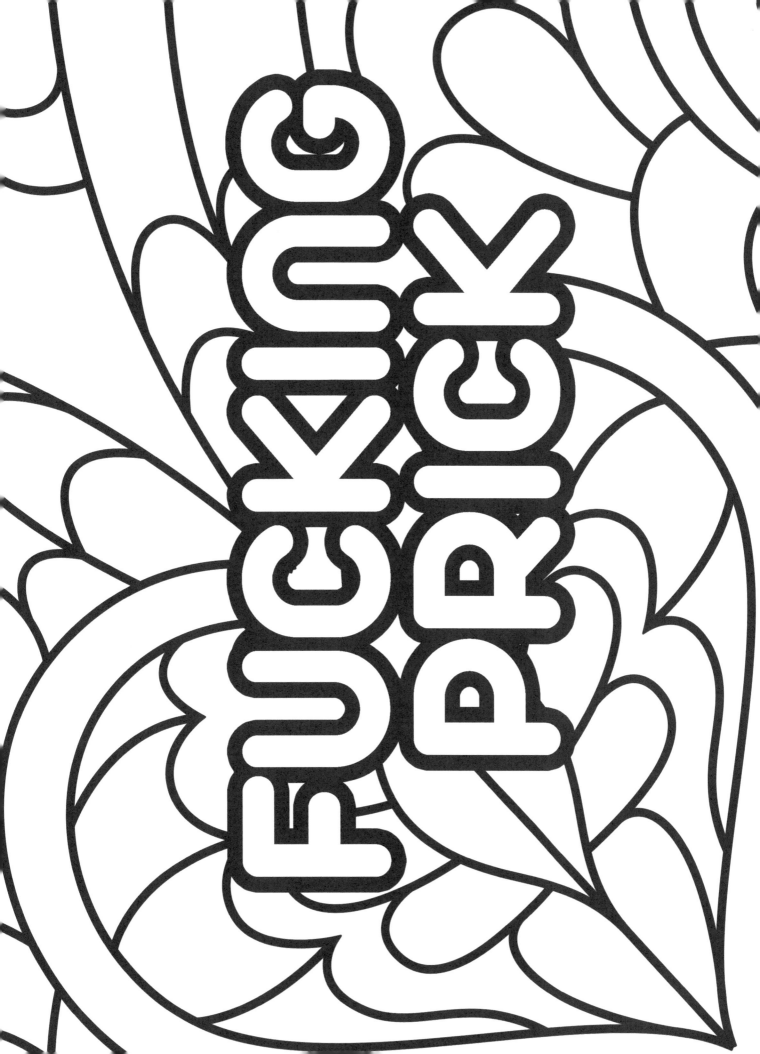

Made in United States
Troutdale, OR
10/07/2024

23502773R00051